STORY BY
GAYLE TAYLOR DAVIS

ILLUSTRATIONS BY
LYN MEREDITH

WILD AND CURIOUS ATTICUS JAMES

AT THE GNU PETTING ZOO

Atticus James at the Gnu Petting Zoo

Hardcover ISBN: 978-1-943050-69-7
Paperback ISBN: 978-1-943050-70-3
November 2017

Barn Owl Media is a wholly owned imprint of HBE Publishing

All inquiries should be addressed to:

HBE Publishing
640 Clovis Ave
Clovis, CA, 93612

http://www.hbepublishing.com

HBE PUBLISHING
Creating alternatives for a creative world

Printed in U.S.A

Dedication:

To my daughter Shea who blessed me with Atticus James — love you bunches!

To Atticus — may you always be wild and curious.

and

To Dan and Lyn, who have wild and curious hearts — thank you for understanding that art loves company.

GTD

To my son Tanner

LM

WILD AND CURIOUS ATTICUS JAMES

At the
Gnu Petting Zoo

Young Atticus James was born to be wild,
Maybe a jaguar or ocelot's child,

although he was born to humans instead.
Still, he was wild inside his head.

His parents would scold him, "now, son, there are rules."
"Just wait, you'll see when you go to school."

And when the time came, for school in the fall
it wasn't too long before they got the call—
"Your Atticus James is a curious child."

Then Teacher added, "he is often quite wild!"
His mom and his dad both replied with a grin,
"Curious and wild? What a place to begin!"

"Let's do begin," Teacher said with a scowl.

Yesterday, he was a great-horned, white owl.

The day before that he was
a huge, green-toed yak,

with sharp pointy ears
and a pink hairy back

"Today, he said, 'I'm a grey wildebeest.'
"He snorted and stomped, then pointed out east,
crying, 'Follow me, class!'" and off they all went.

I'm telling you both, my energy's spent!"

She glanced then, at
Atticus, right where he sat,

He was turned upside down,
saying, "Now, I'm a bat!"

His dad spoke up then, "We do understand, Miss,
We'd be glad to help, if we can, with all this."

The Teacher said softly, though lost deep in thought,
"We don't want his passion to all be for naught.

"Yes, maybe there is something
you both can do,
There's a wonderful place called
The Gnu Petting Zoo.

"Can you take him there,
where the animals are?
I promise you both,
it's not very far."

"Yes! Yes!" cried his parents, each grabbing their hat.
"For goodness sakes, why didn't we think of that?"

Off the car sped,

with a zip and a zoom,

and quickly arrived at Ms. Zenika's room.

Atticus, please, now come with us, son.

Let's go to the zoo, where we all can have fun.

Atticus James followed, with a bounce and a jump,
He smiled at his teacher and did a fist bump.

She watched out the window, and gave a big sigh,
As they boarded the bus, she waved a goodbye.

Once on the bus, they slipped fast to their seat,
Atticus James thought of the wild things to meet.
The bus chugged and whirred, spit exhaust from behind.
It wound past the city and through trees, as it climbed.

Before long it stopped, with a screech and a grate,

and quick dumped them out to a guide at the gate.

To Atticus James he said, "Please, follow me,
for curious and wild is the best way to be,

There's only one rule here,
yes, that is true.
You can pet the animals,
and they can pet you.

Atticus stopped—
he almost fell flat.
They can pet me?
I never thought about that!

But I can pet them,
his wildest heart said,
curiosity and wonder,
filled up his head.

"My name is Gnu,"
the host said, and then smiled,

He opened the gate, saying—

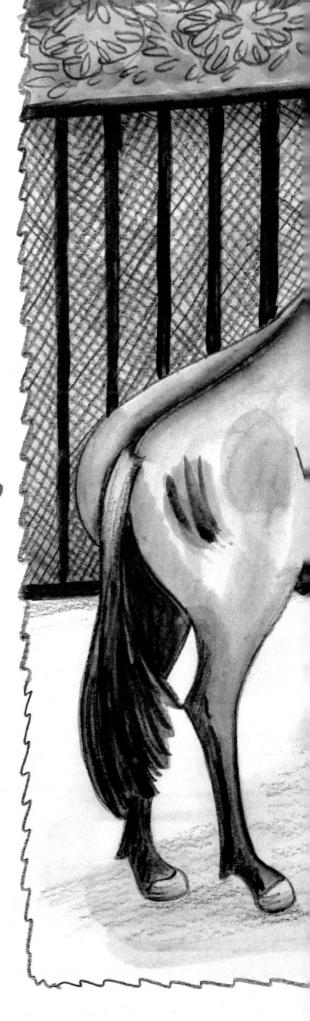

"Welcome to Wild."

So Atticus James gathered all of his brave,
And stepped on the path to a circus parade,
with creatures and animals both curious and wild,
All anxious to see this strange, human child.

"Got the eyes of a badger,"
said a tiny, white bat,

"No, more like a tiger's,"
said a big, ring-tailed cat.

"Is that a hat on his head?"
asked a blue-colored slug,
Then reached out to give his
cowlick a tug.

"That's my hair silly slug,"
he quickly replied,
Then reached out to touch
the slug's slimy side
"What is this goo,
that's all over your skin?"

"It's my sunscreen, you silly,"
Slug said with a grin.

When Atticus James looked up
to the sky,

a spotted giraffe smiled down
and said "Hi!"

He nuzzled his muzzle against the
boy's nose,
giggled and said, "I have spots
just like those!"

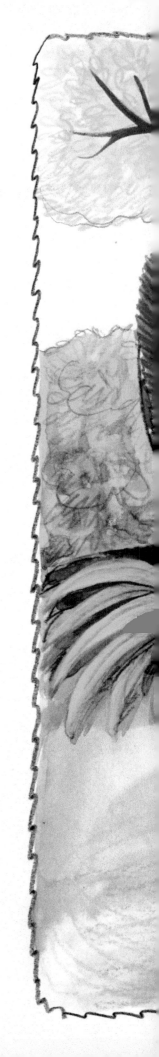

At the thought of his freckles, he just
had to laugh,

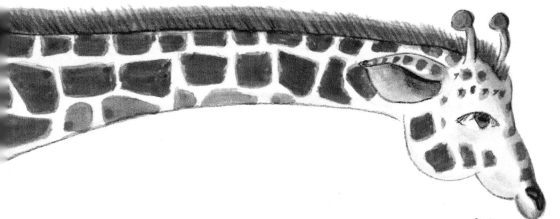

Could it possibly be that I'm part giraffe?

He petted the zebra,
who then counted his
ribs,

saying, "Atticus James,
on stripes I called
dibs."

When Atticus James met a
short kangaroo,

He patted his pouch and said,
"I can hop too."

With all his new friends he went down the path,
'til he spotted a hippo taking a bath,

A rhino,
a cheetah,
a chimp,
and gazelle,
all chatted with him
'til they heard a bell.

"We'd like to talk longer,
but must follow the
rules."
And off they all went to
Wild Animal School.

Back on the bus,
Atticus waved his
goodbyes

"I had the BEST visit
ever," he said with a sigh.

The next day at class, Teacher asked what he thought,
"Animals," he said, "we're more alike than we're not.

But, isn't there something else wilder to see?
Somewhere or some place much wilder to be?"

Teacher tapped on her forehead and thought very hard,

"I know just the place. Here's your
Library Card."

"A library card, Teacher, how can that be?"

"Oh, inside of a book is the wildest

—you'll see!"

About the Author

Gayle Taylor Davis

As a child, Gayle Taylor Davis loved school because that was where the books lived. Those books introduced her to creatures, and people, and places that made her only want to read more books. She loved school so much she decided to become a teacher, so that she could stay in school forever. And she did, almost. One day she thought, wouldn't it be fun to write her own books. So she did.

Gayle taught for 36 years in the Clovis Unified School District, California, where she was twice selected Teacher of the Year by her schools. She is the author of a non-fiction book, "Grief Sucks, But Love Bears All Things". She lives in the Central Valley of California with her husband Dave, their dogs Ricky and Lucy, cat Sophie, and the wild and curious creatures that roam their back pastures (foxes, coyotes, raccoons, possums, and such).

About the Illustator

Lyn Meredith

Lyn, a self-taught artist, lives with her family on a ranch in California. She spends her days riding horses and painting pictures.

Acknowledgments

Behind every writer is a spouse (or cohort) who understands. Every class, every conference, every late night spent writing. In doing so, this patient, giving, supportive person becomes, well — everything. A special thank you to my husband Dave for being my everything.

While writing may seem like a solitary craft, that time alone at the computer is backed by a creative community that teaches, shares, and encourages you each step of the way. I am blessed to have Janice Stevens mentorship through her Writing for Publication Class. Always encouraging and supportive, Janice introduced me to talented children's book authors Karen Moore and Kathy Gorman. They shared their expertise with me, and I have learned so much from them. We have become great writing and traveling buddies, and I am forever grateful. They welcomed me into their Sassy Scribes Critique Group, a wonderful group of authors who provide great feedback. My Friday Writers group, gifted authors Anne Biggs, Susan Lowe, and Kara Nickel Lucas inspire me daily with their work ethic and desire to create magic on the page.

It was Karen and Kathy who introduced me as a writer to Dan Dunklee, my publisher. He and his wife Peggy, owner of A Book Barn in Clovis, CA, are ardent supporters of art and literature in our community. As an editor, Dan has a sharp eye for detail, and can take a piece I've been struggling with, and say, "Try this." He's magic.

I met my illustrator, Lyn Meredith, quite by accident. I spotted her art at Two Sisters Vintage Home and Garden and fell in love. She met Dan and he selected her to be my artist. Her illustrations are filled with beautiful and creative detail. The colors make my heart happy.

This book is mine, and I am grateful, but it really belongs to all these generous people who helped make it become a reality. I thank them with all my heart. Having them as my friends is certainly no accident. God has His hands in everything wonderful that has come into my life. This book and this wonderful group of friends are no exception.

GTD

Teacher's Resources

Atticus James: A Classroom Guide and Support for K Teachers
Common Core State Standards
Flesch-Kincaid Grade Level 1.7

Kindergarten – Use as a read aloud with your class.

Strand: Reading Literature

Key Ideas and Details

K.RL.1

K.RL.3

Craft and Structure

K.RL.4 (wild, scold, curious, scowl, naught, anxious, muzzle, pouch, cowlick, rules)

K.RL.6

Integration of Knowledge and Ideas

K.RL.7

Strand: Reading Informational

Key Ideas and Details

K.RI.1

K.RI.2

K.RI.3

Craft and Structure

K.RI.4 (wild, scold, curious, scowl, naught, anxious, muzzle, pouch, cowlick, rules)

K.RI.5

K.RI.6

Integration of Knowledge and Ideas

K.RI.7

K.RI.8

Strand: Reading Foundational

Print Concepts

K.RF.1

Phonics and word Recognition

K,RF.3.c

Strand: Writing

Text Types and Purposes

K.W.1

K.W.3

Strand: Speaking and Listening

Comprehension and Collaboration

K.SL.1

K.SL.3

Strand: Language

Vocabulary Acquisition and Use

K.L.4.a and b

K.L.5.c and d

First Grade – Use as a read aloud with your class, or a challenge for high readers
Strand: Reading Literature
Key Ideas and Details
    1.RL.1
    1.RL.2
    1.RL.3
Craft and Structure
    1.RL.4
    1.RL.6
Integration of Knowledge and Ideas
    1.RL.7
    1.RL.9

Strand: Reading Informational
Key Ideas and Details
    1.RI.1
    1.RI.2
    1.RI.3
Craft and Structure
    1.RI.4 (wild, scold, curious, scowl, naught, anxious, muzzle, pouch, cowlick, rules)
    1.RI.6
Integration of Knowledge and Ideas
    1.RI.7
    1.RI.8

Strand: Reading Foundational
Print Concepts
    1.RF.1
Fluency
    • 1.RF.4

Strand: Writing
Text Types and Purposes
    1.W.1
    1.W.3

Strand: Speaking and Listening

Comprehension and Collaboration

    1.SL.1

    1.SL.2

Presentation of Knowledge and Ideas

    1.SL.4

    1.SL.5

    1.SL.6

Strand: Language

Conventions of Standard English

    1.L.1

Vocabulary Acquisition and Use

    1.L.4.a (wild, scold, curious, scowl, naught, anxious, muzzle, pouch, cowlick, rules)

    1.L.6

Atticus James: A Classroom Guide and Support for 2nd Grade Teachers
Common Core State Standards
Flesch-Kincaid Grade Level 1.7

Second Grade – Use as a read aloud with your class, or a challenge for high readers

Strand: Reading Literature
Key Ideas and Details
>2.RL.1
>2.RL.3

Craft and Structure
>2.RL.5
>2.RL.6

Integration of Knowledge and Ideas
>2.RL.7

Strand: Reading Informational
Key Ideas and Details
>2.RI.1
>2.RI.3

Craft and Structure
>2.RI.4 (wild, scold, curious, scowl, naught, anxious, muzzle, pouch, cowlick, rules)
>2.RI.5
>2.RL.6

Integration of Knowledge and Ideas
>2.RI.7
>2.RI.8

Strand: Reading Foundational
Fluency
>2.RF.4

Strand: Writing
Text Types and Purposes
>2.W.1
>2.W.3

Strand: Speaking and Listening
Comprehension and Collaboration
>2.SL.1
>2.SL.2

Presentation of Knowledge and Ideas
>2.SL.5
>2.SL.6

Strand: Language

Conventions of Standard English

    2.L.1

Knowledge of Language

    2.L.3

Vocabulary Acquisition and Use

    2.L.4.a (wild, scold, curious, scowl, naught, anxious, muzzle, pouch, cowlick, rules)

    2.L.5

    2.L.6

Atticus James: Teacher's Notes

Part One--Getting Ready

A) Pre Reading Activities (Based on students' interests and abilities.)

1.   Show the cover to the class and read them the title of the book.

2.   Prepare them for the story by talking about:

3.   Then ask the to tell you what they think a gnu might be. This can easily lead into a conversation about what animals they might find at a zoo

4.   Create a class graph of favorite animals.
•   Ask to make predictions what they think the story will be about just by looking at the cover and reading the title of the book.
•   Prompt students to talk about a book they wanted to pick up and read just by looking at the cover and reading the title.

5.   Journal writing prompt. "My favorite zoo animal" or "I like going to the zoo because . . ."

B) Introducing new vocabulary words
   1. Teacher instructions: Listen to the word, listen to the sentence, then let's try to figure out what the word means together.
•   wild: "Young Atticus James was born to be wild."
•   scold: "His parents would scold him, "Now, son, there are rules."
•   curious: "Your Atticus James is a curious child."
•   scowl: "Let's do begin," Teacher said with a scowl."
•   naught: "We don't want his passion to all be for naught."
•   anxious: "All anxious to see this strange human child."
•   cowlick: "Then reached out to give his cowlick a tug."
•   muzzle: "He nuzzled his muzzle against the boy's nose."
•   pouch: When Atticus James met a short kangaroo, he patted his pouch and said, "I can jump too."
•   rules: "Now son, there are rules."

Part Two-During Reading

1. For kindergarten and possibly first grade, use this story as a read aloud asking questions to check for understanding during the reading.

2. For some first grade and most of second grade this story can be used either as a read aloud, small group, or whole group literature read.

3. Comprehension Questions to ask during reading (CFU) or once story has been read:
•   Why do you think young Atticus James likes to act like different animals? Explain why.
•   Why did Teacher call his parents? Explain your answer.
•   Has your teacher ever called your parents? Do you remember why or what you did?
•   There are two settings in this story. List them.
•   Where did Teacher suggest Atticus' parents take him?
•   Have you ever been to a petting zoo?
•   How is a petting zoo different from a public zoo?
•   What did Teacher give Atticus James at the end of the story?

Part Three-Closure (Ideas to help students better understand story structure, sequence of events and character analysis.)

1. Elements of story: identify the main characters

2. Discuss real vs make believe

3. Identify the setting for the story.

4. Identify the problem and the solution.,

5. Bring in personal elements by prompting students to talk about a visit to a zoo. If there are students in your class who have never been to a zoo, take your class on a virtual field trip. Check out You Tube for ideas.

6. Research project for a class or individual students: from list of zoo animals created during the reading of the story, ask students to pick one and research facts. Rather than the typical report project teach students how to create a flip book with one detail and illustration on each page.

Atticus James

Vocabulary Guide

What's another word for?

1. wild—unruly, rowdy, untamed

2. scold—reprimand, lecture, firmly tell

3. curious—inquisitive, nosy, interested

4. scowl—frown or glare

5. naught—nothing or zilch

6. anxious—enthusiastic, eager, excited

7. cowlick—hair, curls, swirls

8. muzzle – nose, snout, mouth

9. pouch – pocket, hole, opening

10. rules—guidelines, laws, directions

Atticus James: A Classroom Guide and Support for Teachers
Vocabulary-- Giving Words Meaning and Giving Meaning to Words
Flesch-Kincaid Grade Level 1.7

This strategy was created to familiarize students with the vocabulary words in a given book or unit being taught. Each step is a guide to help students make sense of the words they come across in their reading.

Step 1-Introduction
a)   write the word on the whiteboard
b)   read the word to the class
c)   ask students to repeat
d)   example "The word is monster. What's the word?" Class responds, "The word is monster."

Step 2-Student friendly definition
a)   teacher states the word, then gives the class word definition
b)   example: "Monster, an imaginary creature that is typically large, ugly, and frightening"
c)   students repeat the definition of the word
d)   when possible the teacher should also show a picture of the word (good strategy for both second language and visual learners)

Step 3-Rephrase the definition,
a)   teacher reads a sentence and students supply the new word.
b)   example "I didn't find a hairy _____ in your closet."

Step 4-Provide other examples
a)   teacher reads the second sentence
b)   teacher demonstrates using Total Physical Response TPR (whenever possible)
c)   teacher illustrates word
d)   as an additional activity to encourage imagination students can also illustrate new vocabulary words. (nouns are easy)

Step 5- Check for understanding
a)   partner time: share the definition with you shoulder partner
b)   tell a time when you . . . .
c)   quiz your neighbor on the new words

CPSIA information can be obtained
at www.ICGtesting.com
Printed in the USA
FSOW04n1851281117
41623FS